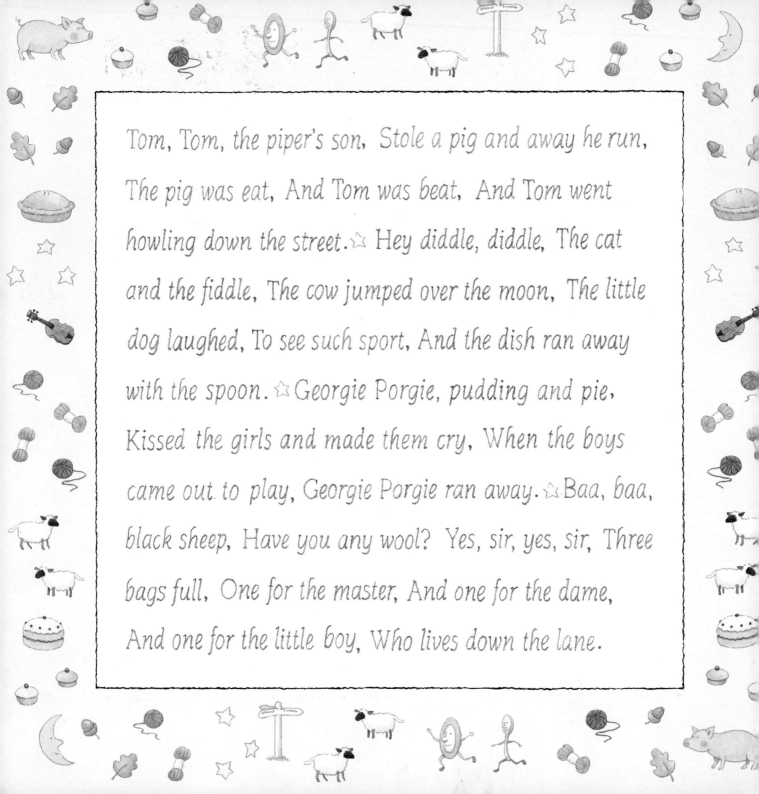

Tom, Tom, the piper's son, Stole a pig and away he run, The pig was eat, And Tom was beat, And Tom went howling down the street. ☆ Hey diddle, diddle, The cat and the fiddle, The cow jumped over the moon, The little dog laughed, To see such sport, And the dish ran away with the spoon. ☆ Georgie Porgie, pudding and pie, Kissed the girls and made them cry, When the boys came out to play, Georgie Porgie ran away. ☆ Baa, baa, black sheep, Have you any wool? Yes, sir, yes, sir, Three bags full, One for the master, And one for the dame, And one for the little boy, Who lives down the lane.

Mary had a little lamb, Its fleece was white as snow,
And everywhere that Mary went, The lamb was sure
to go. ☆ Old Mother Hubbard, Went to the cupboard,
To fetch her poor dog a bone, When she got there, The
cupboard was bare, And so the poor dog had none. ☆
Goosey, goosey gander, Whither shall I wander? Upstairs
and downstairs, And in my lady's chamber, There I met
an old man, Who would not say his prayers, I took him
by the left leg, And threw him down the stairs. ☆ Hickory,
dickory, dock, The mouse ran up the clock, The clock
struck one, The mouse ran down, Hickory, dickory, dock.

First published in hardback in Great Britain by HarperCollins Publishers Ltd in 1999
First published in Picture Lions in 2000

1 3 5 7 9 10 8 6 4 2
ISBN: 0 00 6646778

Picture Lions is an imprint of the Children's Division, part of HarperCollins Publishers Ltd.
Text copyright © Hiawyn Oram 1999
Original ideas and illustrations copyright © Jonathan Langley 1999
The author and illustrator assert the moral right to be identified as the author and illustrator of the work.
A CIP catalogue record for this title is available from the British Library.

The HarperCollins website address is: www.fireandwater.com

Manufactured in China

Where Are You, Little Lamb?

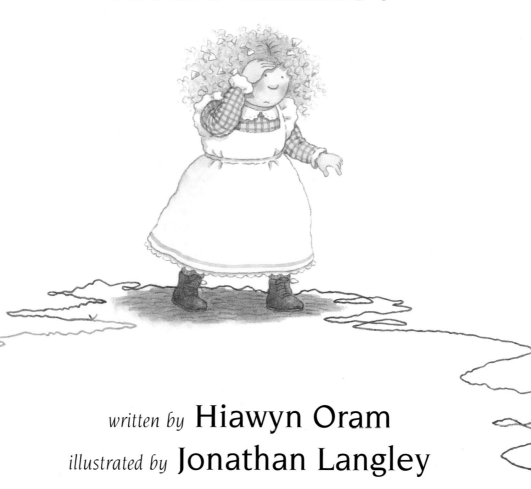

written by **Hiawyn Oram**

illustrated by **Jonathan Langley**

PictureLions
An Imprint of HarperCollinsPublishers

One sunny morning,
Mary woke up early.
"Good morning, Little
Lamb!" she cried.
But Little Lamb did not
answer because Little
Lamb was not in her bed.
"Now, now," said Mary.
"Where are you hiding?"

Is Little Lamb under
the bed?

Is Little Lamb behind
the door?

Mary ran into the farmyard.
"Help! Help! Little Lamb
is missing!"
"Try my fiddle case," said
Cat. "Or over the moon."
"Or in my bags of wool,"
said Black Sheep. "And
don't laugh Little Dog.
It isn't funny."

Is Little Lamb in Cat's
fiddle case?

Or *over the moon*?

Or in *Black Sheep's
bags*?

So Mary, Black Sheep, Cat, Cow, Little Dog and Goosey Goosey Gander ran up the stairs to My Lady's chamber.

Is Little Lamb in the suit of armour?

Or in the sewing basket?

Or in the grandfather clock?

So Mary, Black Sheep, Cat, Cow, Little Dog, Goosey Goosey Gander and the Hickory Dickory Mouse ran over to Old Mother Hubbard's house.

Is Little Lamb behind the curtains?

Or in the laundry basket?

Or in the cupboard?

So Mary, Black Sheep,
Cat, Cow, Little Dog,
Goosey Goosey Gander,
Hickory Dickory Mouse
and Old Mother Hubbard
ran over to the Old
Woman's shoe.

Is Little Lamb behind
the door?

Or up the chimney?

Or through the window?

So they all went up to
Jack and Jill's well on
the way to the Counting
House.

Is Little Lamb down the well?

Or in the King's pie?

Or under the Queen's skirts?

So Mary, Black Sheep, Cat, Cow, Goosey Goosey Gander, Hickory Dickory Mouse, Old Mother Hubbard, the Grand Old Duke, Tom the Piper's Son, and the King and the Queen followed Little Dog all the way back to the farmyard...

...and there,
what do you know,
safe and sound...
they *found* Mary's lamb!

Can *you*?

Jack and Jill, Went up the hill, To fetch a pail of water, Jack fell down, And broke his crown, And Jill came tumbling after. ☆ There was an old woman who lived in a shoe, She had so many children she didn't know what to do, She gave them some broth without any bread, She spanked them all soundly and put them to bed. ☆ Oh, the grand old Duke of York, He had ten thousand men, He marched them up, To the top of the hill, And he marched them down again, And when they were up, they were up, And when they were down, they were down, And when they were only halfway up, They were neither up nor down.

Sing a song of sixpence, A pocket full of rye, Four and twenty blackbirds, Baked in a pie, When the pie was opened, The birds began to sing, Wasn't that a dainty dish, To set before the king? The king was in his counting house, Counting out his money, The queen was in the parlour, Eating bread and honey, The maid was in the garden, Hanging out the clothes, When down came a blackbird, And pecked off her nose. ☆ Little Miss Muffet, Sat on a tuffet, Eating her curds and whey, Along came a spider, Who sat down beside her, And frightened Miss Muffet away.